The Gorgon's Head

The Gorgon's Head

A MYTH FROM THE ISLES OF GREECE

Retold by MARGARET HODGES

Illustrated by CHARLES MIKOLAYCAK

LITTLE, BROWN AND COMPANY

BOSTON   TORONTO

The source of many of our English words, ideas, and stories is the great civilization of ancient Greece, "the Greek Miracle," which sprang up in a land surrounded by many barbarous tribes and people. The Greeks were among the first people to hold human beings in high regard and to envision their gods in human form. Thus they felt close to all of their gods, especially to Zeus, the supreme ruler and the father of Perseus, whose story is told in *The Gorgon's Head.*

LIBRARY OF CONGRESS CATALOG CARD NO. 75-169009

FIRST EDITION

T 03/72

*Published simultaneously in Canada
by Little, Brown & Company (Canada) Limited*

PRINTED IN THE UNITED STATES OF AMERICA

For my friends, the Greeks

"It may be we shall touch the Happy Isles . . ."

T HE gods love a hero. As every day dawns, they show him the path that he must follow, even to the farthest ends of the earth and over the perilous sea. The gods guide him and guard him in danger, and when he dies they take him straight up into the starry heavens. Such a hero was the Greek Perseus, son of the god Zeus.

Perseus lived in danger from the day of his birth, because his grandfather had dreamed that someday the boy would kill him. The old man locked the baby and its mother, Danaë, into a wooden chest and cast the chest into the sea.

But the gods sent gentle winds to calm the sea and waft the helpless voyagers to an island. There, a fisherman drew them ashore and brought them to his king.

Perseus and his mother lived on that island in the king's palace until the boy was fifteen years old and eager for heroic deeds. Then the king desired Danaë for his wife, and when she refused him, vowed to make her his slave. This he could not do so long as Perseus was near.

"If you are truly a hero," said the wily king, "go to Greece and bring back the head of Medusa. She is one of the Gorgons, who are monsters with teeth like swine, sharp claws of bronze, and powerful golden wings for giving chase to their victims."

Boldly, Perseus set off. Sailing to his native land, he climbed a high cliff above the sea and prayed the gods to guide him. As he prayed, a cloud appeared before him and in the cloud he saw Athena, goddess of wisdom, clad in flowing robes and bearing a bright shield. Beside her stood Mercury, messenger of the gods, in the guise of a young man with a winged helmet and winged sandals. He carried a shining sword.

As if she knew the hero, Athena asked, "Do you dare to meet Medusa?"

Perseus answered, "I dare anything."

Athena was pleased. "Now listen well," she said. "The Gorgon's head is covered with hissing snakes, and her face is so horrible that whoever looks at it is turned to stone. Take my polished shield, and when you approach Medusa, look only at her reflection in the shield."

"Take my sandals," said Mercury, "for you must travel first to the back of the North Wind, where the Three Gray Sisters live. They have only one eye among them, but with that eye they can see the farthest parts of the earth, and they know the way to Medusa's home. Take my sword, too, for it is magic and will quickly slay the monster." He fastened his winged sandals on the feet of the hero.

Perseus took the sword and the shield in his hands. Then, trusting his life to the gods, he leaped from the cliff and borne by the winged sandals high above the blue sea, sped northward, until he found the Three Gray Sisters in the land of the long, dark night.

The old women sat huddled together, their thin, gray hair blown by the North Wind, while one of them, with the wonderful eye in her forehead, told the others everything she was seeing in countries far away. But at last another said, "Sister, it is my turn to use the eye. Give it to me."

And the third sister wailed, "No, it is my turn."

The one who had the eye begged, "Let me keep it a little longer."

Then they began to quarrel, until the one with the eye was forced to take it out of her forehead. Now, at that moment, all three of the sisters were blind, and Perseus stepped close to them. As they groped about, passing the eye from hand to hand, he held out his own hand, and one of them put the cold, shining eye into it, thinking that it was the hand of her sister.

"I have the eye," cried Perseus, "and I will throw it into the sea unless you tell me how to find the Gorgons."

They wept and scolded and shook their gray heads, but they were afraid to lose the eye. At last they said, "Go to the islands where the sun shines all day long, and find the nymphs who guard the apple tree in the garden of the gods. They will help you and guide you on the last part of your journey. Now give us back our eye."

Then Perseus gave back their far-seeing eye and flew away southward until he came again to blue waters and saw below him many islands, golden in the sun. Here he searched. At last he heard the sound of singing and saw an island where the water nymphs danced around an apple tree of gold in the garden of the gods. The nymphs were kind to Perseus. They told him the way to the island of the Gorgons and they gave him a magic pouch which would stretch to hold whatever he put into it. Then they put on his head a cap of darkness to make him invisible, and he vanished from sight.

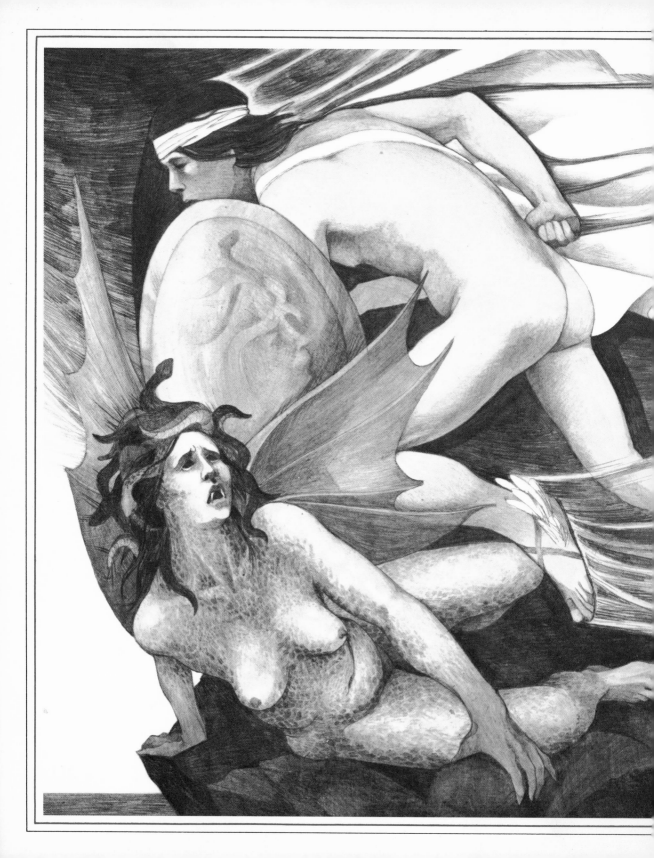

Now was the time to prove himself a hero. Borne on by his winged sandals, he saw the Gorgons' isle far below and heard the rustle of their wings. He held the shield above his head and looked up at its polished surface.

There Perseus saw the reflection of the Gorgons, with their hard serpent scales, their long tusks and claws of bronze. Their golden wings were folded, for they were asleep. Perseus poised in midair. Then he flew down and down.

Now he could see clearly in his shield Medusa herself, with a tangle of serpents twisting upon her head. Swift as a seabird he came down, and with one sweep of his sword, cut off that monstrous head. Then he lifted it by its snaky locks, put it into the magic pouch, and rose up into the air.

But now the Gorgon sisters awoke. They saw Medusa's headless body. Howling for revenge, they sprang into the air, looking for him who had slain their sister. Guided by the hissing of snakes, they followed Perseus.

But the winged sandals carried him higher than their heavy golden wings could fly, and the cap of darkness covered him. At last their howls died away on the empty air.

Now, far out over the sea on his homeward journey, Perseus looked down and saw a lovely maiden, her gentle body bound with cruel chains to a rock, while a sea monster in the rough waves at her feet made ready to devour her.

"I have never seen so beautiful a maiden," thought Perseus. "Surely she is a king's daughter."

Then he took off the cap of darkness and she saw him. Down from the sky he shot like a meteor. "Close your eyes," he cried, and she obeyed. Turning his head aside and holding the Gorgon's head before him, Perseus flew close to the waves. One look at Medusa, and the monster lay still, an island of stone in the sea.

Perseus tore away the chains that bound the maiden to the rock, asking, "Who are you and what cruel man bound you here?"

"My name is Andromeda," she said. "My father is the king of this island. The sea-gods sent their monster to destroy all of us, and the people forced my father to chain me to this rock, so that the monster might devour me and spare them."

But Perseus said, "Now you belong to me." And he flew away with Andromeda in his arms until he came to his own island and entered the king's palace.

The king turned red with anger when he saw Perseus. He had expected the Gorgons to tear the young man to pieces.

"Have you brought me the head of Medusa?" he asked. "If not, you shall die."

Then Perseus answered, "Behold the Gorgon's head!" and he drew it out of the magic pouch.

The king looked upon that hideous face, and his own face grew pale. He sat very still. And there he sits to this day, a cold, gray stone on a lonely island in the sea.

But Perseus returned to the land of his birth, and the people, seeing that he had a royal heart, made him their king. For many years he ruled well, with fair Andromeda as his queen. And when their days on earth were ended, the gods lifted them up into the sky to shine forever among the stars: Andromeda, the gentle princess, and Perseus, the hero, holding in his hand the Gorgon's head.